On the edge

No way out

Mike Gould

Folens

© 2003 Folens Limited, on behalf of the author.
United Kingdom: Folens Publishers, Apex Business Centre, Boscombe
Road, Dunstable, LU5 4RL.
Email: folens@folens.com

Ireland: Folens Publishers, Greenhills Road, Tallaght, Dublin 24.
Email: info@folens.ie

Poland: JUKA, ul. Renesansowa 38, Warsaw 01-905.

Editor: Kay Macmullan
Layout artist: Lee Williams
Cover design: Duncan McTeer
Illustrations: Josephine Blake

First published 2003 by Folens Limited.

British Library Cataloguing in Publication Data. A catalogue record for
this publication is available from the British Library.

ISBN 1 84303 394–1

Contents

1   Mel's bar   5

2   The letter   10

3   Money for nothing   16

4   Taking action   19

5   A visitor calls   22

6   The loan   25

7   Dedlock's   28

8   Back at the bar   35

9   That Friday feeling   39

The story so far

If you haven't read an *On the edge* book before:
The stories take place in and around a row of shops and buildings called Pier Parade in Brightsea, right next to the sea. There's Big Fry, the fish and chip shop; Drop Zone, the drop-in centre for local teenagers; Macmillan's, the sweet and souvenir shop; Anglers' Haven, the fishing tackle shop; the Surf 'n' Skate shop and, of course, the Brightsea Beach Bar.

If you have read an *On the edge* book you may have met some of these people before.

Mel Slater :   *Aussie, runs the 3 Bs bar.*

Sandra King: *works in the 3 Bs bar and is married to Frankie.*

So, what's been going on?
Mel Slater came half-way across the world to open the 3 Bs. But after the storm it took him time and money to rebuild it.

What happens in this story?
Mel is unusually slow to open his bar one morning and Sandra wonders why. There's quite a story behind his behaviour, however, and Sandra is keen to investigate.

1

Mel's bar

An Australian named Mel owned the
Brightsea Beach Bar.
It was in Pier Parade, between the fish and
chip shop, and the Surf 'n' Skate shop.
Most people called it the 3 Bs.

Nobody knew how old Mel was.
Some said he was fifty.
Some said he was thirty.
If you asked Mel, he would just laugh and
say, "You're as old as you feel!"

Most mornings he opened the bar at
about 11.30 am.
He would fold back the big shutters from
the window. He would then pull out
the large awning, like on a tent, which
provided shelter from the sun, or the rain.

But this morning, the shutters were
closed, and the awning hadn't appeared.

Nobody knew why.

Mel always opened the bar.
The 3 Bs was open every day of the week
in the summer.

Sandra King knocked on the door
and waited.
But there was no answer.

Sandra was a part-time waitress at
the bar.
She liked to get out.
Being stuck in her terraced house all day
was bad news.
Her husband, Frankie, told her to use
their new flat at the marina, but she
didn't like it there.
They weren't her sort of people.
She liked Mel, and she liked working
for him.

"Mel!" Sandra shouted. "It's me!"

She wondered if he had overslept.
But that too would have been
very unusual.
Mel loved getting up early.
He never overslept.

"Mel? Are you all right?"

She banged on the door again.

Then she heard the scrape of a chair, and
weary footsteps.
She heard the bolt sliding back.
The door opened.

Mel had not shaved, and he looked tired.
He didn't say anything, but just walked
back into the bar.
He went behind the counter, and started
to dry the the coffee cups and put them
on to the racks.

"Mel, what's the matter?"

Sandra put down her handbag.
She took off her jacket, and hung it on the
coat stand.
She had never seen Mel look like
this before.

Mel still didn't say anything, but he did
put down the cup he was drying.
Then he picked something up from the
counter, and held it out to her.

It looked like a letter.

2

The letter

"Read it," Mel said.

On the envelope was an
Australian stamp.
The letter was rather crumpled.
Mel must have read it many times.

Cairns, 15ᵗʰ June

Dear Mel,

I am so sorry.
*I couldn't face phoning you to tell you
the bad news.*

It's Little Joe.
His boat is missing off the coast.
*No one has heard from him for three
weeks.*

We all fear the worst.
The weather looked so good when he left
and there's been no storm, so no one
knows why he has gone missing.

I know what you did for Joe, and I want
you to know how grateful he was.

Please don't feel you have to catch the
next plane over.
There is nothing you can do.
If there is any news I will let you know
straight away.

All my love,
Auntie Marg

Sandra passed the letter back to Mel.

"Who is Little Joe?" asked Sandra.
"I grew up with Little Joe in Australia,"
said Mel. "We were like brothers. His
name was a joke really. He wasn't little at
all. Little Joe is ... was ... six feet six, and
built like a tractor."

"Is he your cousin?"

"No. His mum took me in when …" Mel paused.

"Go on," said Sandra.

"That's another story," said Mel. "It doesn't matter now. All that matters is that Little Joe isn't here anymore."

"So, what's happened? What does she mean about the boat? Is he a fisherman?"

Mel slumped down in a chair by one of the tables.
He'd picked up another coffee cup, and was drying it for the fourth or fifth time.

"Ever since I first met him, Little Joe loved sailing. He really knew how to handle a boat. He loved sailing almost as much as he loved nature and wildlife, especially sea creatures. He always dreamed of discovering a new type one day, and having it named after him. 'The Little Joe Fish' he used to joke."

Mel smiled at the memory.

"When I was young he used to take me out on his boat. He taught me to deep-sea dive."

"And now he's disappeared?"

"The sea is pretty rough out there."

"But the letter said the weather was good."

Mel shook his head.
"Maybe. But it's been three weeks. Three weeks without hearing."

Sandra got up and started to open the shutters.
The news was bad.
It sounded as if Mel and Little Joe had been close.
But it was unlike Mel to give up like this.
He was always the hopeful one.

"There's nothing you can do, Mel. Your aunt said …"

Mel suddenly got to his feet.
The cup fell from his grasp on to
the table.
It shattered into pieces, and showered the floor by Sandra's feet with tiny splinters.

"You don't understand, Sandra. That's not everything."

"What do you mean?"

"It's not just Little Joe disappearing."

Mel looked down at the tiny fragments.

Then his voice softened.

"I'm sorry, Sandra. I shouldn't have lost my cool like that. It's just difficult to bear. You see, it's not just about Little Joe. It's me. I'm ruined."

3

Money for nothing

Outside, people were beginning to arrive at Pier Parade.

Macmillan's was already open.
Early morning holidaymakers were coming in and out of the shop, clutching little gifts, or sticks of rock.

Next door, Ken Woodley was leaving the fish and chip shop.
He was off for his morning drive to the cash and carry.

"I should be going to the cash and carry too," said Mel. "But I can't face it."

Sandra went and sat next to Mel at the table.

"Tell me what you meant, Mel," said Sandra. "About being ruined."

Mel explained.

"That trip Little Joe was on. It wasn't any ordinary fishing trip. Little Joe was searching for a rare species of fish. One that can only be found very deep down, on the ocean floor. It is a beautiful and special fish. Unique. He had persuaded an Australian television company to make a documentary about it. But he had to find the fish first. On his own. That's what he was doing when he disappeared."

Sandra looked puzzled.

"But how does that affect you?"

"Little Joe had no money. And neither did Auntie Marg. So, I offered him the money – as a sort of loan. You see, Little Joe needed a special boat, special camera equipment and special diving gear. It wasn't cheap. He was going to pay me back when he returned."

Sandra still looked puzzled.

"So, you're out of pocket. No big deal, is it?"

Mel looked at her.

"I really wanted to help Little Joe. The problem is, I owe money on this bar. Lots of money. I borrowed money to buy it and my bank has told me I must pay them back. If not, they will take the bar from me. Close the business."

4

Taking action

Sandra leapt into action.

"Come on, Mel. We can't let this happen. The bar has to open in an hour's time. If you don't open today, people will realise what's going on, and never come back."

She grabbed the broom, and started sweeping up the broken cup.

"But it's hopeless," argued Mel. "Whatever happens, I still owe the money."

The phone suddenly started ringing.

"Shall I answer it?" said Sandra, stepping towards the phone, which was on the end of the bar.

"I don't know. It might be bad news."

Mel moved towards the phone, but as he reached over the counter, it stopped.

"Let's not worry about that now," Sandra said. "Get yourself a shave. And put on a clean shirt. You've got a bar to run."

Mel turned, and sloped off to the washroom at the back of the bar.

Sandra swept up the remainder of the
broken pieces, and then opened
the shutters.

The sun slanted in from the east, across
the front of the bar.
It lit up the computer screens at
the side.

The bar had two computers for any
customers who wanted to send emails.
Mel used them to contact old friends
in Australia.
Sometimes Mel had asked Sandra to open
his emails for him.
She even remembered the odd message
from someone called 'LJ'.
It must have been Little Joe.

She dusted off the screens and keyboards,
and then turned both machines on.
She wasn't much good with computers
– but she knew the basics.

5

A visitor calls

Half an hour later, Sandra was wiping the surface of the last of the outside tables, when a shadow fell across it.

"Is Mr Slater in?"

Sandra looked up.
A tall, rather pale woman stood in front of her.
She was wearing a dark blue trouser suit, and looked a bit like a funeral director.
She held a slim, black briefcase.

"Who are you?" asked Sandra.

"I have private business with Mr Slater."

"Did you phone earlier?"

The woman ignored her.
"Is he in?" she asked again.

"No …" Sandra lied.
"He's …" she hesitated for a moment.
"… at the cash and carry."

"Ah. I see," said the woman. "Here's my card."

"Tell him to call us. Today."

Before Sandra could say anything, the woman had disappeared.
Like a ghost.

The card read:

Ms Ursula Dedlock

Associate Director
Dedlock's Loan Agency Ltd
10 Fleetside Road
Brightsea BS4 2GE

Sandra placed the last few chairs in position, and then went back into the bar.

6

The loan

"Has she gone?"

Mel crept out from behind the bar.

"Yes," answered Sandra. "Who is she?"

"That's Miss Dedlock, part of the Dedlock family. They run a small agency that gives business loans."

"I thought you said it was a bank?"

"Well, it is a sort of bank," said Mel sheepishly. "That's how they described it."

"Why did you use them?"

"They were the only ones that would lend me the money when I came to England. The big banks wouldn't look at me. The problem is, Dedlocks charge very high interest rates. Even so, I'm close to paying off the loan. All I needed was another month. The bar has been going really well. Then Little Joe asked me to lend him money. I couldn't refuse. We were like brothers."

Sandra paused.
She was thinking.

"Can I pop out for a moment? Before the bar opens. I'll only be twenty minutes."
"Of course you can."
"Somehow we'll get you out of this mess."

Sandra walked over to Mel, and gave him a light kiss on the cheek.

"What was that for?" Mel said, blushing.

"You looked like you needed cheering up."

Sandra rubbed the lipstick mark off
Mel's cheek.

"Not a word to Frankie, mind!" she said,
and turned and left the bar.

Mel felt his face where Sandra had
kissed it.
But before he could think about it, the
first set of customers came in.

He moved behind the counter, and
waited for them to come over.

7

Dedlock's

Sandra had expected a posh-looking
office in the town centre.
But when she found the place it was
rather different.
It was in a narrow side street.
There was no sunlight, and it was
unusually quiet.

There was a small plaque on the wall.
There were several businesses listed, but
the one at the top read 'Dedlock's Ltd'.

She climbed the musty stairs to the top
floor, and knocked on the panelled door.

No one answered, so she pushed it.

It was locked.
She sighed, and was about to go.

Suddenly, the door opened, and a small
man hurried out.
He looked around secretively, as if he
didn't wish to be seen.
Quickly Sandra stepped inside before the
door shut again.

It certainly wasn't like a bank.
There was a long, narrow corridor with
doors off to the sides, but they were
all closed.

At the end she could hear the sound of
a voice.

She walked along the corridor until she
came to another door.
It was half open.
Beyond the door Miss Dedlock was on
the phone.
Sandra halted.
She could hear what was being said.

"This is your last chance. Of course, if you can't pay I'm sure my brothers could drop by to see you. What's that? You didn't enjoy their last visit? You must have said something to upset them. No, a cheque won't do. Cash only. You have twenty-four hours."

Sandra heard the woman put the phone down.

Then she knocked on the door.

"What is it, Mr Watts? I have already told you …"

Sandra entered the room.

Miss Dedlock looked at her.
"Not Mr Watts, I see. Do you have an appointment?"

"I don't need one. I'm here on behalf of Mel."

Miss Dedlock placed the tips of her fingers together and leant forward on the desk.

"And who might 'Mel' be?"
"Mel Slater," replied Sandra.

"Ah, yes. Mr Slater. A serious case. Owes
us quite a lot of money. I wasn't aware he
was married."
"He's not. I'm a friend. I work for him."

Miss Dedlock laughed.
It wasn't a pleasant sound.

"Well, I think you had better start looking
for another job. If Mr Slater does not pay
his monthly sum by the end of the week,
the bar will be ours."

Sandra could feel the anger rising
inside her.

"Do you realise the work he's put into
that place? The hours painting it, cleaning
it? It was a real dump when he bought it.
Now it's one of the best bars on
the seafront."

"I'm sure it is," said Miss Dedlock in a bored voice. "And I'm sure when we sell it, we'll get an excellent price."

Sandra took a step towards the desk.

For the first time Miss Dedlock looked a little shaken.

"You need to give him more time. The bar is going really well. He'll have paid his debts by the end of the month."

Miss Dedlock sighed.

"I'm afraid it's against company policy to extend the loan period. If the money isn't ready by Friday, I will be forced to send my brothers …"

Sandra interrupted her.

"Oh yes, I've heard all about your brothers. I heard you threatening someone on the phone. And that poor little man who just left. Mr Watts? Was he one of your victims too? Will he be getting a visit from your brothers?"

For a moment Miss Dedlock seemed lost for words.
Then she regained her composure.

"I have no idea what you mean. My brothers are perfectly entitled to collect any debts."

She stood up.
Her pale face on her thin neck made her look like a scrawny hen.

"Now, please leave my office. Or I shall have to call security."

Sandra turned and headed for the door. But before she left she had one more thing to say.

"You'll get something by Friday. I promise you that."

8

Back at the bar

Sandra did not tell Mel where she had been.

"You were gone an hour. I thought you said twenty minutes."

"Something came up," she told him. "I'm sorry. I'll work extra hours later in the week."

Mel looked gloomy.

"Don't bother. On Friday, the bar will no longer be mine."

"Perhaps something will turn up. You never know," said Sandra.

"The only thing likely to turn up is that terrible woman. Do you think they'll rename it 'Dedlock's Bar'? Mind you, I can't imagine her working here. She'd drive the customers away."

They both laughed at the thought.

"I need to ask you another favour," said Sandra.
"Go on," said Mel.
"I can't come in tomorrow morning. I've got something I must do."
"What is it?"

"Family business," Sandra replied.

"I'm sorry," said Mel. "Didn't mean to pry. No, it's OK. We're not usually so busy Thursday lunchtime."

Sandra took Mel's place behind the bar.

"Have a break," she said. "I can cope with this bunch."

Customers by the bar were laughing and
joking, and ready to order fresh rolls
and sandwiches.

Mel went over to one of the computers.
"How strange!"
He was staring at the computer screen.
"Look at this," he said.
It was a message without a title.
But it did have an attachment.

He clicked on the icon, and a
picture opened.
It was bizarre.
The picture seemed to show the wing of a
plane, or a long oblong shape with a blue
stripe down it.
It was only low resolution, and
very small.

"What is it?"
"I don't know," said Mel.

"Who is it from?"
"I don't know that either. The address
isn't one I recognise."

It read 'IMCook'.

"Do you know anyone called 'Cook'?"
"I don't think so. It must have been sent
by mistake."

With that, Mel pressed 'Delete'.
The message disappeared from his screen.

9

That Friday feeling

All day Mel and Sandra had waited for the Dedlocks to call.
But they hadn't turned up.

Not during lunchtime, when young office workers came in for a bite to eat.
Not during the early evening, when people stopped on their way home from work to sit on the patio outside, in the evening sun.
Not even during the busy night session when the bar was packed with teenagers and students, who preferred it to the pubs.

Now it was 11 pm.
Mel had just closed the bar.

Two customers remained in the corner,
with half-finished coffees in front of them.

"I'm afraid we're closed now, gentlemen,"
said Mel.
"We're just finishing," said one of the
men, taking a quick sip from his cup.

At that moment, the door opened and
Miss Dedlock entered.
With her were her two brothers, wearing
baseball caps, jeans and T-shirts.
They didn't look like bankers.

"We're closed," said Mel.

"How right you are," said Miss Dedlock,
placing her briefcase on the table.

"I assume you do not have this month's
payment, nor last month's … nor the
month's before?"

Mel bowed his head.
"No."

Miss Dedlock opened the briefcase.
She pulled out a set of papers.

"In that case, you'll be prepared to sign these documents. They give over ownership of the bar to us."

Sandra, who had been watching from behind the counter, came forward. "Don't sign them, Mel!"

The two brothers stepped forward.
They didn't say anything.
They didn't need to.

"What choice do I have? They'll take it anyway."

"Wait a moment," said Sandra. "Let me ask Miss Dedlock a few questions first."

Miss Dedlock looked at her for the first time.

"Is it possible for people to own a business when they have criminal convictions for threatening people? Is it legal to let people take out loans without telling them exactly what the terms are?"

"What are you talking about?" said
Miss Dedlock.

Sandra pulled an envelope out of
her pocket.
Then she opened it, and let the contents
spill on to the table.

Out fell several photos, and a
tape cassette.

The photos showed the Dedlock brothers
and the small man, Mr Watts, whom
Sandra had seen at the office in town.
One of the brothers held his collar.
The other brother was entering a house.
There were other photos, too, of the
Dedlock brothers at other houses and
flats, doing similar things.

"I suppose you're wondering what's on
the tape?" said Sandra.

Miss Dedlock said nothing.

"Well, after I left you, I found Mr Watts in the street. He was still shaking.
I persuaded him to carry a tiny tape recorder on him for your brothers' next visit. I also decided some photos might help. So yesterday, I took time off work to do a little detective work."

Miss Dedlock scowled.
"Who's going to believe a few grubby photos and a tape? Anyone could make that lot up."

"Actually, we are," said one of the men in the corner.
Mel had forgotten all about them during the conversation.

"I'm Detective Sergeant Routledge," said the taller man. "And this is my colleague DC Leavis."

"When Mrs King came to see us, it wasn't much of a surprise. We already knew about you and your brothers. But it did make us decide to look at your activities more closely."

Mel looked astonished.
"You're police officers?"

DS Routledge smiled.

"Yes. Nice little bar you've got here.
I'd like to come back when I'm off
duty sometime."

He turned to Miss Dedlock.
"I wonder if you and your two brothers
would mind popping into the station
tomorrow? About 10 am. We have a
number of questions we'd like to ask you.
And I think you should leave Mr Slater
alone for tonight. Now's not the time for
doing business."

For a moment the Dedlocks didn't move.
Had the photos and the tape been a waste
of time?

Then, Miss Dedlock snapped her
briefcase shut.
"Come on," she said to her two brothers.
"This can wait."

She gave Mel and Sandra one, final nasty look as she left, followed by her brothers.

Mel looked at Sandra.
"You were fantastic! And thanks for being here, guys," he added, gesturing at the two officers. "Can I offer you another drink?"

"No thanks. We'll be on our way."

The two men headed for the door, but before they left, the larger man spoke.

"Make sure you lock up carefully. I wouldn't put it past a certain family to make a return visit."

As the door shut after the police officers, one of the computers beeped.
Sandra went over to it.

"Mel," she called, "I think there's something you should see."

The message read:

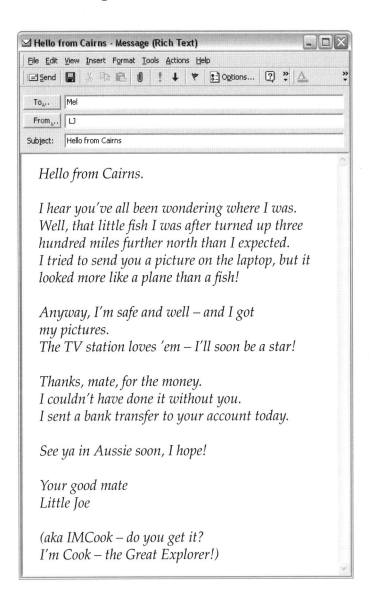

Hello from Cairns - Message (Rich Text)

File Edit View Insert Format Tools Actions Help

Send   Options...

To..:   Mel

From..:   LJ

Subject: Hello from Cairns

Hello from Cairns.

*I hear you've all been wondering where I was.
Well, that little fish I was after turned up three
hundred miles further north than I expected.
I tried to send you a picture on the laptop, but it
looked more like a plane than a fish!*

*Anyway, I'm safe and well – and I got
my pictures.
The TV station loves 'em – I'll soon be a star!*

*Thanks, mate, for the money.
I couldn't have done it without you.
I sent a bank transfer to your account today.*

See ya in Aussie soon, I hope!

*Your good mate
Little Joe*

*(aka IMCook – do you get it?
I'm Cook – the Great Explorer!)*

Mel looked astonished.

"I should have guessed. Captain Cook
– he discovered Australia. Anyway, the
main thing is he's safe – and I've got my
bar back! This calls for a drink!"

He went behind the counter and pulled a
bottle of champagne out of the fridge.
He popped it open.

Sandra joined him at the counter.
They held up their glasses of golden,
fizzy liquid.

"To Little Joe!" said Sandra.

"To Little Joe and you!" said Mel.

Lost in their celebrations, Mel and Sandra
failed to notice the figure in the shadows.
For a minute, it stood watching them
through the bar window.
Then it turned abruptly and melted into
the darkness.